E NAGEL

Nagel, K.
Shapes that roll.

PRICE: $14.99 (21742/jp/M

KAREN NAGEL

SHAPES THAT

Text copyright © 2009 by Karen Nagel   Illustrations copyright © 2009 by Steve Wilson

All rights reserved. CIP Data is available. Published in the United States 2009 by

Blue Apple Books, 515 Valley Street, Maplewood, NJ 07040

www.blueapplebooks.com

Distributed in the U.S. by Chronicle Books

First Edition

Printed in China

ISBN: 978-1-934706-81-7

10 9 8 7 6 5 4 3 2 1

ROLL

illustrations by
STEVE WILSON

blue apple books

and **SQUARE**.

CIRCLE,

Follow the

TRIANGLE,

Follow them **HERE**.

Follow them **THERE**.

Follow them **HIGH**.

Follow them **LOW**.

UP and **DOWN** to the places they'll go.

They'll
show you
shapes
that **SLANT**, **STACK**, and **ROLL**.

Shapes that are **HALF**, shapes that are **WHOLE**.

Shapes that are **ROUND**

Shapes with **8 SIDES**.

Let these
three different shapes
be your expert shape guides.

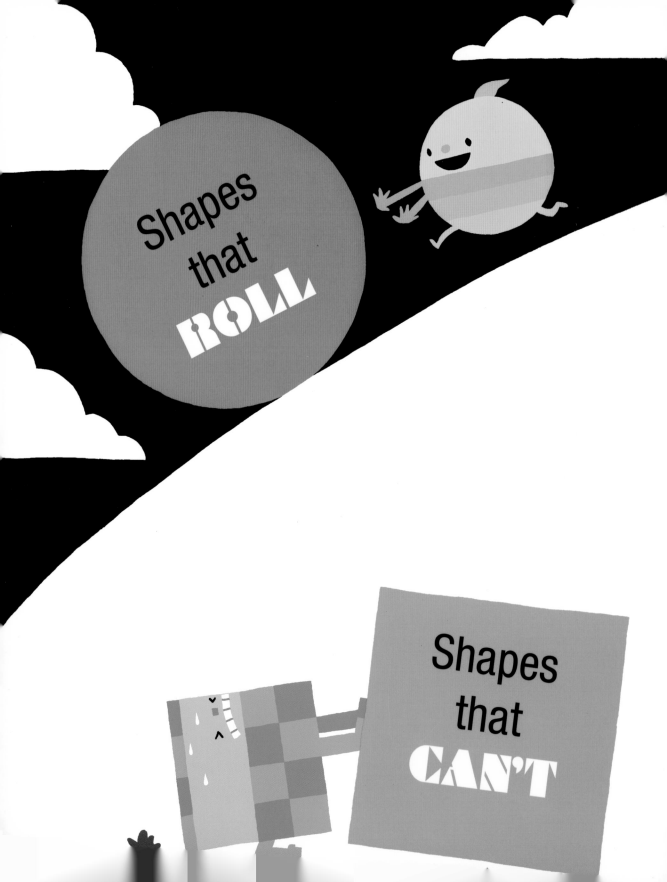

Shapes
that
ROLL

Shapes
that
CAN'T

Shapes
with
sides
that
angle
and
SLANT.

Some
shapes
STACK

Some
shapes
DON'T

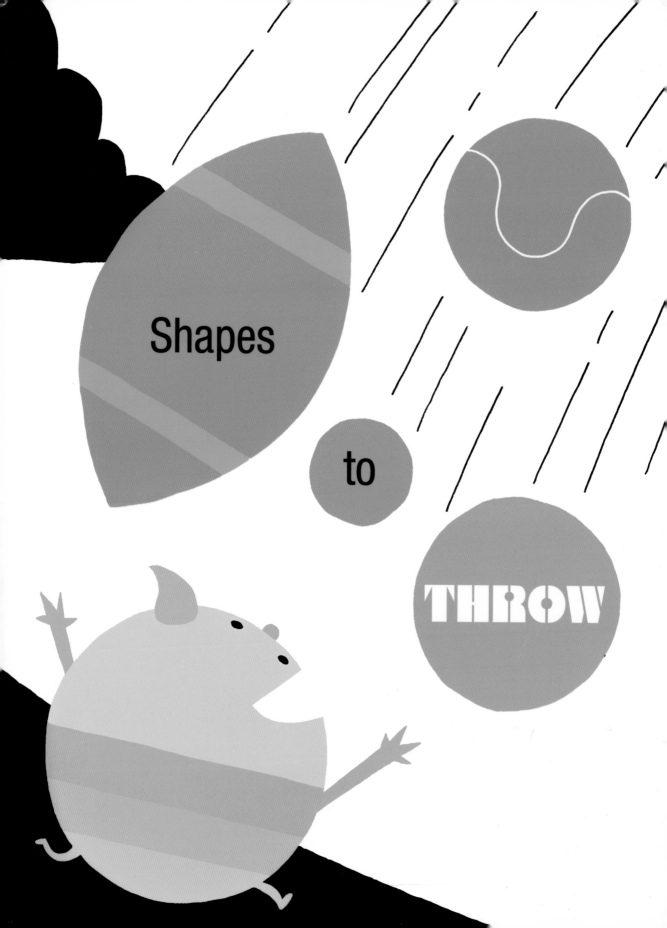

Shapes to THROW

Shapes to
SHARE

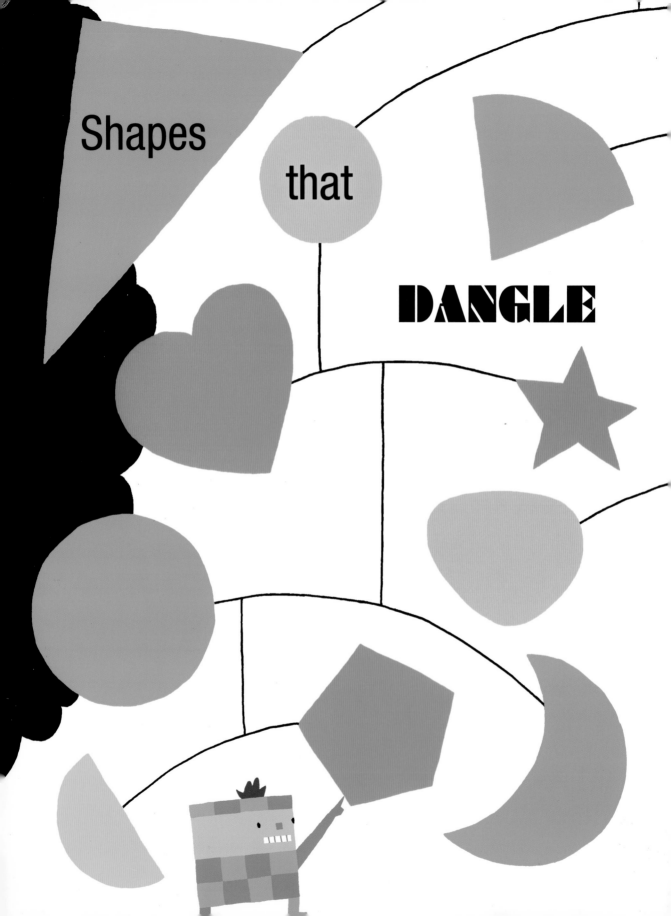

Shapes that DANGLE

in

the
AIR.

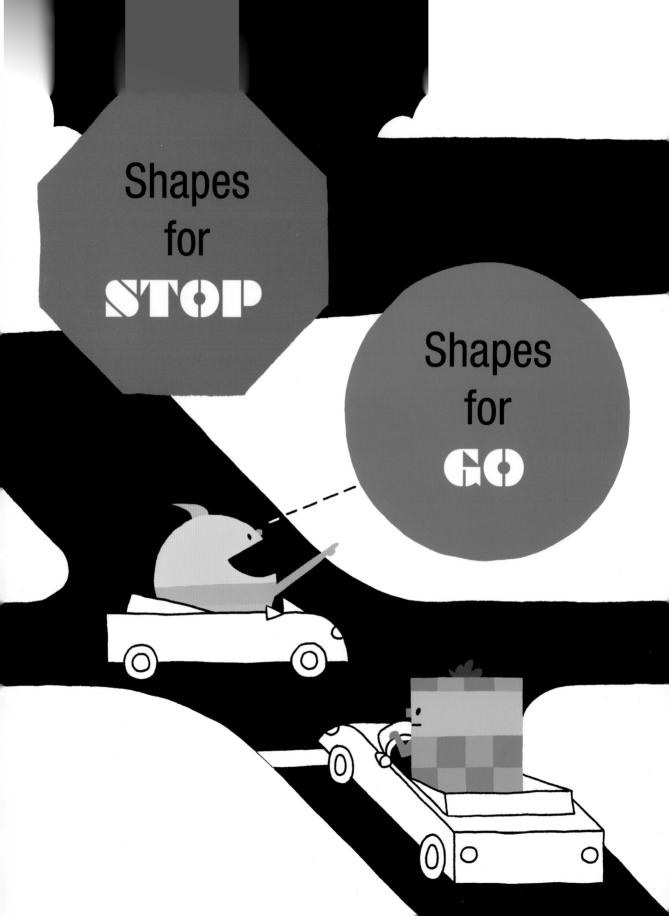

A house

has
many
shapes

to **SHOW**.

Shapes that SHINE

Shapes that FREEZE

Shapes
of fruits

that
grow
on

TREES.

Shapes
that
glimmer
up
ABOVE

Shapes
that
make you
think of
LOVE.

Shapes to **OPEN**

Shapes to **CLOSE**

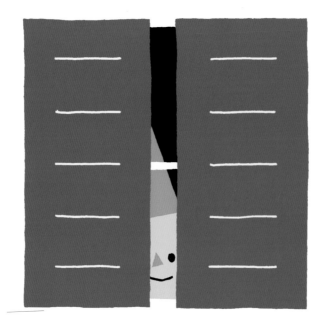

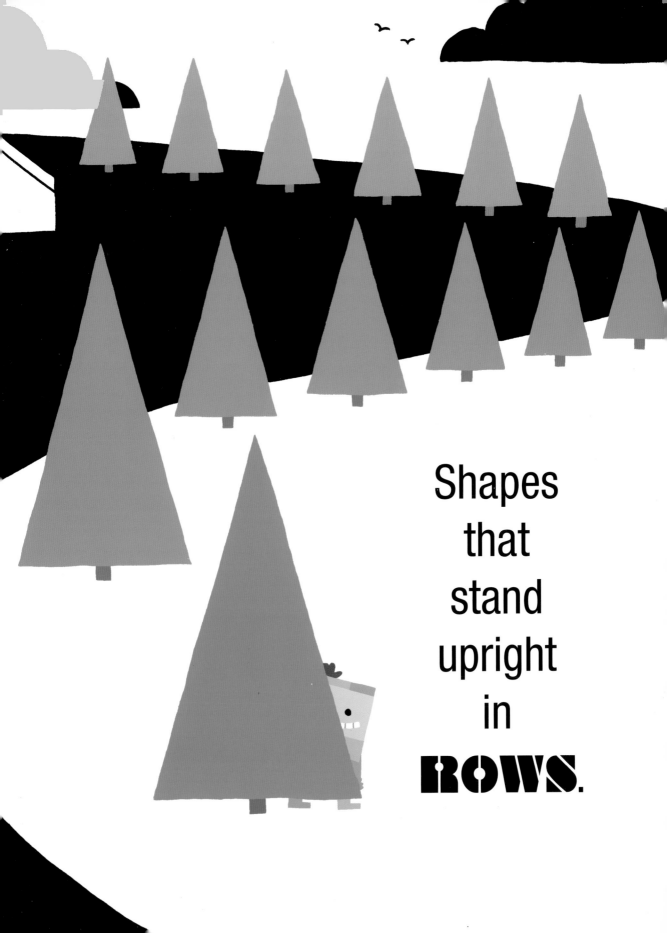

Shapes
that
stand
upright
in
ROWS.

Shapes that TEETER

Shapes that PLAY

Shapes
help
people
find their
WAY.

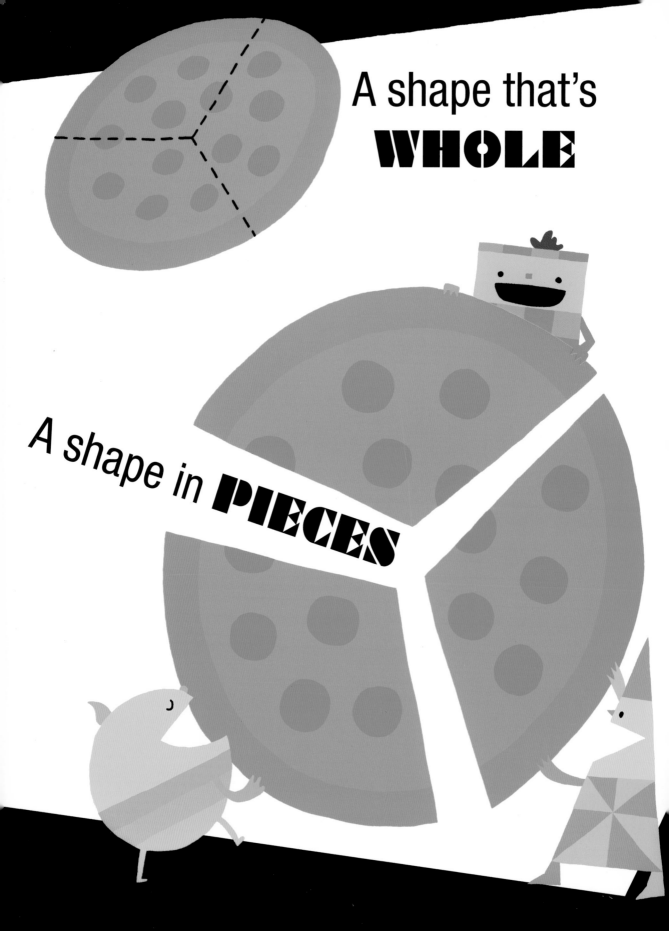

A shape that's
WHOLE

A shape in **PIECES**

Shapes
with many folds and
CREASES.

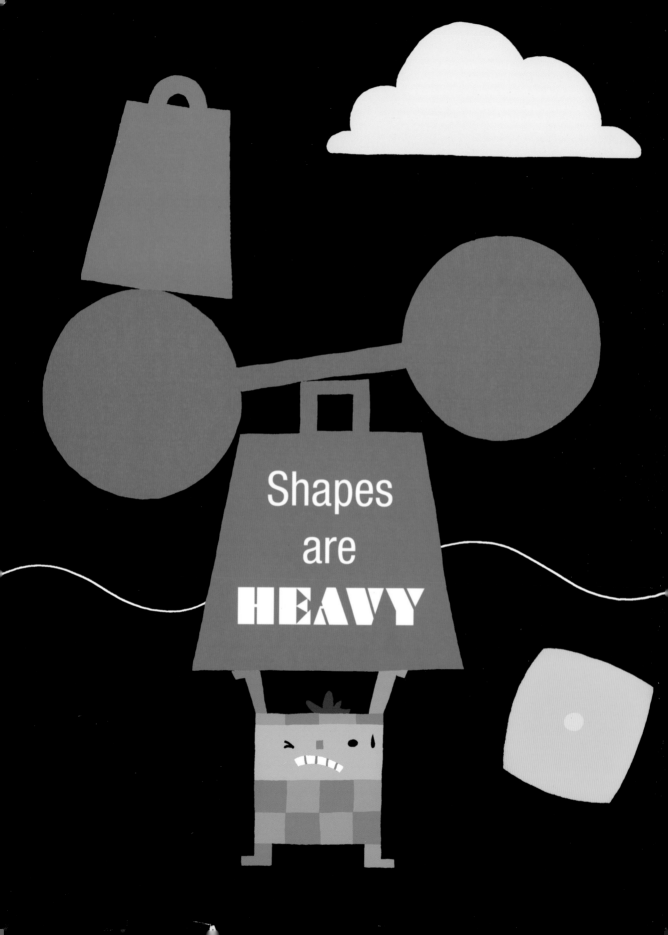

Shapes are **HEAVY**

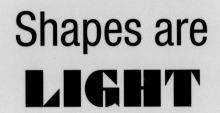

Shapes are
LIGHT

Pillow shapes
are sure to
FIGHT.

Squares
LIE
DOWN

Did you see the arrows,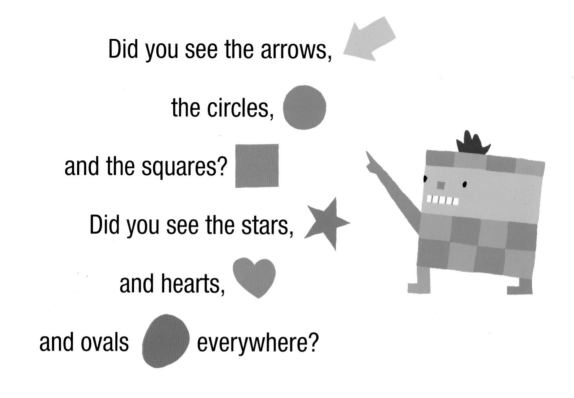
the circles,
and the squares?
Did you see the stars,
and hearts,
and ovals everywhere?

Triangles,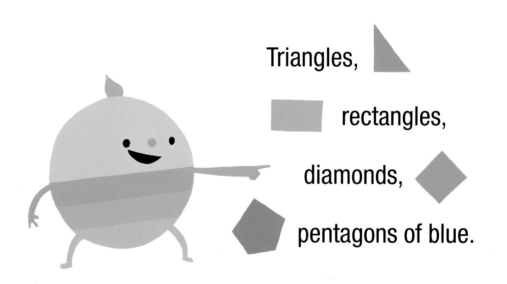
rectangles,
diamonds,
pentagons of blue.

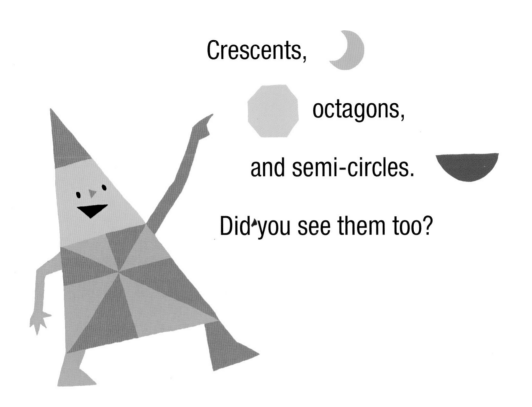

Crescents, octagons, and semi-circles.

Did you see them too?

SHAPES

of every size and kind

are found inside this book.

The whole wide world

is made of shapes. . .

they're
EVERYWHERE
you look!